Sir Mouse
to the Rescue

This edition first published in 2012
by Book Island, Raumati South, New Zealand
info@bookisland.co.nz

Text © Dirk Nielandt
Illustrations © Marjolein Pottie
English language translation © Laura Watkinson 2012
English language edition © Book Island 2012

Original title: Muis en Draak - Help! Help!
© Uitgeverij De Eenhoorn Wielsbeke 2012

A catalogue record for this book is available from the
National Library of New Zealand.

Edited by Gillian Tewsley and Frith Williams
Typeset by Vida & Luke Kelly, New Zealand
Printed by Everbest, China

The publication of this book has been made possible with the
financial support of the Flemish Literature Fund.

ISBN: 978-0-9876696-2-9

Visit www.bookisland.co.nz for more information about our books.

MOUSE & DRAGON
an unusual friendship

Sir Mouse to the Rescue

by **Dirk Nielandt and Marjolein Pottie**

Translated by Laura Watkinson

BOOK ISLAND

Mouse has a sword.
She wears a suit of armour.
She is a knight.
She is bold Sir Mouse.

Dragon does not have a sword.
She does not wear a suit of armour.
She is just Dragon.

Knights fight dragons.
But Mouse and Dragon never fight
each other.
Mouse and Dragon are best friends.

ABOUT A TALL TALL TOWER

Mouse and Dragon hear someone shouting,
"Help! Help!"
Who's that crying for help?
Who's in danger?
"Help! Help!" they hear again.
Mouse looks at Dragon.
"What should I do?" she says.
Her voice is trembling a little.

"Are you a knight?" Dragon asks.
"Of course I am," Mouse says boldly.
"I have a sword. I have a suit of armour.
So I am a knight. I am bold Sir Mouse."

"And what do knights do when someone
calls for help?" Dragon asks.
"They help," Mouse replies.

Then they hear the shout again. "Help! Help!"
"Do you know what I'm going to do?" Mouse says
boldly. "I'm going to help!"

Mouse and Dragon follow the shouts.

They come to a castle.
The castle has a tall, tall tower.
Mouse and Dragon look up.
At the top of the tower, they see Prince at a window.

"Help! Help!" Prince shouts.
"How do you want me to help you?" Mouse shouts
up to Prince.
But Prince can't hear her. "Help! Help!" he cries again.

"Ooh, that's so annoying," Mouse says.
"What is?" Dragon asks.
"He just keeps shouting *Help! Help!* all the time."

"Help! Help!" Prince shouts again.
"See what I mean?" Mouse grumbles. "I can't help him
if he just keeps shouting for help."
"Why not?" Dragon asks.

Mouse sighs and says, "How does he want me to help him?
What does he want me to help him with?
He didn't shout anything about that, did he?
Maybe he needs some help with his homework.
Or he's looking for someone to tidy his room.
Or he can't find his football.
Or he could be sitting on the loo and he's run out of paper."

"Help! Help!" cries Prince.
"That's not what it sounds like," says Dragon.
"Well, what does it sound like?" asks Mouse.

Dragon thinks for a minute.
"It sounds like he's in danger.
Maybe he's locked up in the tower.
Maybe he wants to be rescued."

Mouse looks up.
"Do you know what?" she says boldly. "I have an idea.
I'm going to rescue him from that tower."

And that is exactly what Mouse does.
She looks up at the tall, tall tower.
Prince's window is very high.
It's going to be a long climb.
"I need a rope," says Mouse. "Or a ladder or a crane.
Something like that."

"Maybe I can rescue Prince," says Dragon.
Mouse bursts out laughing. "Don't be so silly," she says.
"You are Dragon, not a knight. Do you ever read books?"
"No," Dragon admits.
"Exactly," says Mouse. "Who rescues the prince in books?"
"Um ..." Dragon says.
"It's always the knight, never the dragon," says Mouse.

Dragon hangs her head in shame.
"I'm sorry," she says.
"That's okay," says Mouse.

HELP

HELP! HELP! HELP! HELP! HELP!

HELP! HELP! HELP!

Mouse looks around.
"Where can I find a rope? A nice, long rope?"

"Help! Help!" Prince shouts again.
Mouse sighs.
"Just *listen* to him!" she says. "We're doing our very best
to help, and all he can do is shout *Help! Help!*
He just keeps complaining."

"Help! Help!" shouts Prince.
"Stop that shouting," Mouse yells at Prince.
"Or you'll just have to help yourself.
You're really starting to get on my nerves."

"Help! Help!" Prince shouts again.
Mouse has had enough.
"Come on," she says to Dragon. "We're going home.
I can't stand all this shouting."

"But what about poor Prince?" says Dragon. "We can't
just leave him, can we?"
"It's not my fault," says Mouse. "We don't have any rope.
It's tough luck for Prince.
But I wish he'd stop going on and on."

"I have an idea," says Dragon. "I'm very big and tall.
I'll lift my head up to the window, and Prince can
slide down my neck."

"No, wait!" Mouse cries boldly. "I have an idea.
I can climb your neck,
all the way up to Prince's window,
and I can rescue him from the tower.
Then I'll be the one who saved him."
"Good plan," says Dragon.

And so Mouse and Dragon rescue Prince from the tower.
Prince is very happy.

"Why were you shouting *Help! Help!*?" Mouse asks Prince.
"I read a book," Prince replies. "It was about a prince
who got locked up by a wicked witch."

Mouse pulls out her sword.
"Where is the witch?" she yells.
"There is no witch," says Prince. "I wasn't locked up.
I just thought that being rescued sounded like fun."

Mouse puts her sword away.
"Just give me a shout if you ever need rescuing again,"
she says. "That's what knights are for.
But if you do, don't just shout *Help! Help!*
Shout something like: *Help! Help! Rescue me from the tower!*
Or: *Help! Help! I've run out of loo paper.*"
Prince promises to do his best.

Sometimes, when you want something,
you have to say so very clearly, thinks Mouse.
That always does the trick.
Or at least it usually does.

ABOUT CAT AND CHOPPING FRIENDS INTO PIECES

Mouse is walking through the forest.
Suddenly she hears a twig snap.
Then she hears a rustling sound.
She turns around.
Did someone just jump into the bushes?
Is she being followed?

Mouse takes out her sword.
She walks over to the spot where the twig snapped.
Mouse is not scared.
She is brave because she is a knight.
She is bold Sir Mouse.

But then someone
jumps out from
behind a tree
and grabs her.
It's Cat!

Mouse waves her
sword around.
She jabs Cat.
"Ow!" Cat shrieks,
and she lets Mouse go.

Cat licks her wound.
Mouse points her sword at Cat.
Cat is wearing a suit of armour.
Cat has a sword too.
"Are you a knight?" asks Mouse.
Cat nods.

Mouse puts her sword away.
"Knights don't attack other knights. Don't you
know that?" she says.

Cat shrugs. "I was just in the mood
for a tasty snack," she says.
"Well, you can forget that idea!" Mouse says.
She glares at Cat. "I am not a tasty snack.
I am a knight. I am bold Sir Mouse."

"All right. Then I'll leave you alone," says Cat.
"On your honour?" Mouse asks.
"On my honour," Cat says with a sigh.

Mouse nods.
A knight's word of honour is to be trusted.

"What are you doing here?" Mouse asks.
"I'm on a dragon hunt," says Cat. "If I see any dragons,
I will chop them into pieces."
"With lots of blood and stuff?" Mouse asks.
"With lots of blood and stuff," Cat replies.

"Hello there," says a voice behind them.
Cat and Mouse turn around.
It's Dragon.
Dragon smiles at Cat.
"Nice to meet you," says Dragon.
Then she turns to Mouse.
"Is this a friend of yours?" she says.

But Cat pulls out her sword.
"I will chop you into pieces," she yells at Dragon.
"With lots of blood and stuff!"
Dragon gasps. She doesn't want to be chopped into pieces.

Cat waves her sword around.
"Stop!" Mouse commands.
Cat stops waving her sword and stares at Mouse.
"There'll be no chopping anyone into pieces here,"
says Mouse.
"Why not?" asks Cat. She sounds very surprised.
"That dragon is mine," Mouse replies.
Dragon gasps again. What did Mouse just say?

"I saw that dragon first," says Cat.
"Didn't," says Mouse.
"Did," says Cat.
"Didn't," says Mouse. "I saw Dragon yesterday."

"I don't believe a word of it," says Cat.
"Well, it's the truth," says Mouse.
"So why didn't you chop her into pieces right then?"
Cat asks.
"Because Dragon wanted to brush her teeth before
the fight," says Mouse. "She wanted to make herself
look beautiful. She didn't want to be chopped
into pieces right away."

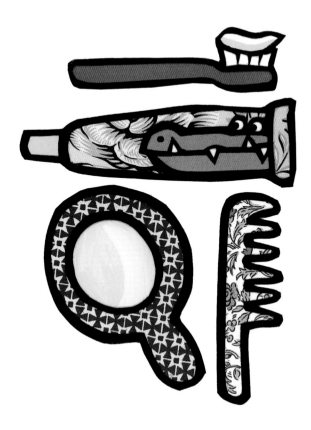

Cat looks at Mouse as if she doesn't quite believe her.
Dragon doesn't have a clue what's going on.
Does Mouse really want to chop her into pieces?
With lots of blood and stuff?
But they're supposed to be friends!

"All right, then," says Cat. "Chop her into pieces!"
"Now?" asks Mouse.
"Now," says Cat.
"Here?" asks Mouse.
"Here!" says Cat.
"With lots of blood and stuff?" asks Mouse.
"Of course. With lots and lots of blood and stuff!"
says Cat.

Mouse sighs.
Then she takes out her sword.
She points it at Dragon.
Dragon is scared. She looks nervously at Mouse.
Does her friend really want to chop her into pieces?

Mouse jumps up onto Dragon's tail.
She climbs all the way up to Dragon's head.

Then she whispers in Dragon's ear.
"I'm sorry. I have to chop you into pieces."
"Why?" whispers Dragon.
"Cat is a knight, like me.
If I don't chop you into pieces, she'll tell everyone.
Then no one will believe I'm a knight."

Dragon understands now.
Mouse wants to impress Cat.
Knights like to impress one another.

"Get on with it!" Cat calls from below.

"Just a moment," Mouse shouts back down to Cat.

"What's taking so long?" asks Cat.

"Stop complaining," Mouse says. "Dragon is
about to fall down dead at your feet.
Watch out or she'll fall on top of you."

Then Mouse whispers in Dragon's ear,
"Just pretend you're dead. Pretend it's a game."
Dragon likes games.
She giggles with delight.

"Why is that dragon giggling?" asks Cat.
"The dragon's not giggling," says Mouse. "I'll count
to three. Then Dragon will die."

Dragon gets ready to fall down dead.
"Aaaargh, I'm dead," Dragon roars with a big grin
on her face. She loves playing dead.

"Wait!" Mouse snaps. "First I have to count to three."
"Sorry," says Dragon.
Mouse counts. "One … two … three!"

Dragon falls down with a heavy THUD.
Cat jumps out of the way just in time.

Mouse jumps down from Dragon.
She puts her sword away.
"Dragon is dead — as a dodo," says Mouse.
"Well done," Cat says.

Cat looks at Mouse, full of admiration.
"Are you going to chop her into pieces?" she asks.
"I'll do that later," Mouse says.
"Why later?" Cat asks.
"First I want to take a picture of Dragon,"
says Mouse. "For my photo album.
It's full of all the dragons I've ever defeated."

Cat looks at Mouse with even more admiration.
"And then you'll chop her into pieces?" she asks.
"Of course," says Mouse.
"With lots of blood and stuff?" asks Cat.
"With lots and lots of blood and stuff," says Mouse.
"Really?" asks Cat.
"Really," says Mouse.

Dragon can hardly stop herself from laughing.
What a fun game!

Cat nods. "You are a brave knight," she says to Mouse.
Mouse beams with pride.
Of course she already knew that,
but it's always nice to hear it from somebody else.

ABOUT REAL AND PRETEND KNIGHTS

Mouse steps into Dragon's cave.
She's been invited to a party.
"Hello, I'm here," she calls.
There is no answer.
Where's Dragon? Mouse wonders.

Suddenly Dragon jumps out at Mouse.
She is wearing a suit of armour.
She has a sword.
"I am Sir Dragon!" Dragon roars.
She waves her sword around.
"I will chop you into pieces!"

Mouse pulls out her sword.
"Come closer," she says boldly. "And I'll chop YOU
into pieces!"
Mouse waves her sword around too.

Dragon laughs.
"Do you like my costume?" she asks.
Mouse glares at Dragon.
"Are you fighting me or not?" she asks.
"Are you crazy!" says Dragon. "It's only me!"

Mouse is not going to stand for anyone calling
her crazy. She jabs Dragon's toe with her sword.
"Oww!" yelps Dragon.
A big fat drop of blood spurts out of Dragon's toe.
Dragon looks at the blood. She gulps.
"That hurt," she says.

"Are you a knight or not?" asks Mouse.
"Not really," says Dragon.
"I thought as much," says Mouse. "You look
far too much like Dragon."

"Don't you like it?" Dragon asks glumly.
Mouse stares at Dragon in amazement.
Not only does Dragon *look* like Dragon,
she *sounds* like Dragon too.
Mouse knows that voice very well.

"You should be ashamed," says Mouse angrily.
"You aren't a knight. You're just Dragon."
"I know," says Dragon.
"So why did you say you were a knight?" asks Mouse.
"I'm just dressed up as a knight," says Dragon. "Where's
your costume?"

Mouse looks at Dragon as if she's crazy.
"Why would I wear a costume?" asks Mouse.
"For the fancy dress party. You have to dress up,"
says Dragon.
"That's silly," says Mouse.

"This is a fancy dress party," says Dragon. "Everyone has to wear a costume. I've come as a knight. Don't you think my suit of armour looks lovely? I'm just like a real knight, aren't I?"

"There's only one knight here," Mouse says sternly, "and that's me!"
Dragon nods. "But it's a shame you didn't wear a costume," she sighs.
"Why would I dress up as a knight?" says Mouse.
"I already *am* a knight."
"Oh, you don't understand," says Dragon.

Mouse is not going to stand for that.
She always understands everything.

She grabs her sword.
She points it at Dragon and cries, "Defend yourself!
Prove yourself a knight or I will chop you into pieces!"

Dragon gasps. "I don't want to fight," she says.
"You see," says Mouse. "That means you're *not*
a knight. Knights always want to fight."
"I never said I *was* a knight," says Dragon.

Mouse glares at Dragon.
"You are wearing a suit of armour," she says.
"You have a sword in your hand.
So you *are* a knight."
"No, no, no," says Dragon quickly. "I'm just
pretending. For the fancy dress party."

Pretending to be a knight?
Mouse has never heard anything so crazy.
Either you're a knight, or you're not.

Dragon pulls off her suit of armour.
She feels very ashamed.
She didn't know that knights don't dress up
for fancy dress parties.

"This is a fun fancy dress party," says Mouse.

Dragon nods.
But she still thinks something's not quite right.
It's a fancy dress party, but no one is wearing
a costume.

Dragon decides not to say that to Mouse.
She doesn't want to make her friend angry again.
Sometimes it's okay when your friends don't want
to dress up. Especially when they're real knights.

ABOUT KNIGHTS AND HAPPY EVER AFTER

"Help! Help! Rescue me from the tower!" cries Prince.
"There he goes again," Mouse says with a sigh.
"Are we going to rescue him from the tower?"
asks Dragon.
Mouse grumbles. "He's making a habit of this.
He can just use the stairs to come down."

"Help! Help! *Please* rescue me from the tower!"
"He's asking very politely," says Dragon.
Mouse sighs again.
"Oh, all right, then," she says. "I'll do it."

Mouse and Dragon go to Prince's castle.
Mouse stands on Dragon's head.
She helps Prince to climb out the window.
Prince slides down Dragon's neck.
Mouse has rescued Prince from the tower again.

"Next time you should just take the stairs,"
says Mouse. "We have other things to do."
"Will you marry me?" Prince asks Mouse.

"We have to defeat enemies," says Mouse,
"and save the king, and defend the land.
And sometimes we need to go shopping
and clean the house …"

"Will you marry me?" Prince asks again.
Mouse doesn't answer. She just goes on talking
as if she didn't hear Prince's question.
"We are busy, busy, busy," she says.

Dragon interrupts her with a little cough.
Mouse stops talking and looks at Dragon.
"What is it?" asks Mouse.
Dragon puts a claw up to her lips to tell Mouse
to be quiet for a moment.

"Will you marry me?" Prince asks again.
Mouse looks at Prince as if he's gone crazy.
"WHAT??!!" she yells.

"Will you marry me?" says Prince.
"Marry? Me? And you?" says Mouse.
"Yes," says Prince.
"Why?" asks Mouse.
"Because it's in all the books," says Prince.

Mouse stares at him with her mouth wide open.
Prince opens up a book.
He shows Mouse a picture.

It's a picture of a knight rescuing a prince.
And then they get married.
And then they live happily ever after.

Prince opens up another book.
That book also has a picture of a knight
rescuing a prince. And they get married
and live happily ever after in that book too.

Prince shows Mouse lots and lots of books.
They always get married!
They always live happily ever after.

Mouse looks glum.
"So the knight always marries the prince?"
Prince nods.

That evening, Mouse is very quiet.
"Why are you so quiet?" Dragon asks.
"I don't know if I want to get married," says Mouse.
"Don't you want to live happily ever after?"
asks Dragon.
"Of course I do," replies Mouse. "But I am a knight.
I am bold Sir Mouse. And if I marry Prince, I'll be Princess."

Dragon says, "Doesn't that sound like fun?
A princess lives in a big castle.
A princess has servants who do as she commands.
A princess wears posh dresses."

Mouse sighs.
"A princess does not wear a suit of armour," she says.
"A princess has no sword. A princess is not a knight.
                    Can you see me wearing a posh dress?"
                        "It might look lovely on you," says Dragon.
                        Mouse sighs.

                    When Dragon has gone home,
                        Mouse tries on a posh dress.
                        She stands in front of the mirror.
                        Ridiculous, thinks Mouse.

Early the next morning, Prince knocks at her door.
"So, are you finally going to marry me?" he asks.
"No," says Mouse. "I want to live happily ever after.
But I don't want to be Princess.
I wear a suit of armour. I have a sword.
I am a knight. I am bold Sir Mouse."

Prince shrugs. "Well, if that's what you want," he says,
"but will you still come and help me when I need
rescuing from the tower?"
"Of course," says Mouse. "Knights always rescue
the prince from the tower. That's what knights do.
It says so in your books."
Prince is happy with that.

Later, Dragon comes around for a cup of tea.
"I know what it says in all the books," Mouse says
to Dragon. "But I'm sure you can live happily ever after
without getting married."

Dragon feels very relieved.
Mouse in a posh dress! she thinks.
And she bursts out laughing.

"Why are you laughing?" asks Mouse.
"Because I'm so happy you're not married,"
says Dragon. "I'd rather have a knight as a friend
than a princess."

And Mouse and Dragon *are* friends!
Best friends forever!
No prince will ever change that.
They're sure of it.
In fact, they're absolutely certain!

ABOUT WAR AND ABOUT FRIENDSHIP

Mouse has made up her mind.
She has packed.
Her rucksack is full.
She is ready to leave.

Dragon looks glum.
"How long are you going to be away?" she asks.
"I don't know," says Mouse. "Maybe forever."

Dragon is shocked.
Forever? That's such a long time.
She is going to miss her friend so much.

"Do you really have to go?" Dragon asks.
Mouse nods. "I am a knight," she says.
"Knights go on long journeys.
Knights conquer countries for their king.
They go out in search of adventure.
They fight battles."

Dragon gasps.
"Battles?" she asks.
Mouse nods.

"But battles are dangerous,"
says Dragon. "You can get
hurt in a battle.
You can be wounded.
You can even die."

"I'm not going to die in a
battle," Mouse says boldly.
"I will defeat every enemy
with my sword."

Suddenly Mouse feels like
she's standing in the shower.
Water is splashing all over her.
She's soaking wet.
*Where's all that rain
suddenly coming from?*
she wonders.

As soon as Mouse looks up, she realises.
Dragon is crying.

"I'm sorry," says Dragon. "I'm just so sad
you're leaving."
"I understand," says Mouse. "I'd be sad too."

Dragon suddenly has an idea.
"Can I come with you?" she asks.
Mouse shakes her head. "I'm sorry, but no,"
she says. "A knight and a dragon can't go out
adventuring together. It just wouldn't be right."

"What am I going to do without you?" asks Dragon.
"You're my best friend.
You help me when I need it.
You're there for me when things get tough.
You listen when I talk to you.
I'd be lost without you."

Mouse nods.
"I know," she says. "But there's nothing
to be done about it. I have to go now. Farewell!"

Dragon glares at her.
"You are abandoning me," she says. "That's not nice.
That's not what friends do – especially not knights."

"Isn't it?" asks Mouse.
"No, it's not!" says Dragon.
"Not even to go into battle?" asks Mouse.
"Not even to go into battle," says Dragon.

"I have an idea," says Mouse. "I'll just stay at home.
Knights don't abandon their friends.
Not even to go into battle."

Dragon grins all over her face.
She picks Mouse up and gives her a huge hug.
"You're a hero," she says.

Mouse nods.
She already knows that, of course.
But it's the sort of thing that needs to be said
and written as often as possible.

MOUSE IS A HERO.
Look, there it is again.
In black and white.
In a book.
Now the whole world knows.
That's nice, isn't it?
Don't you agree?